What It Means to Be a Big Brother

Lindsey Coker Luckey

It's cool to be a father or a mother,
but what does it mean to be a big brother?

I've never been the older sibling before,
but I'm sure it won't be a bore.

There are so many things we will do,
and here are just a few.

I'll cuddle you tight and wish you
a very good night.

I'll feed you a yummy snack
and give you a ride on my back.

I'll teach you, little sibling, how to crawl
and curl up into a tiny ball.

We'll be the best of friends,
but this isn't where it ends!

I'll teach you how to stand on your feet,
then give you candy as a tasty treat.

We'll walk side-by-side with a wiggle,
then I'll chase you around as we giggle.

Then I'll teach you how to ride a tricycle,
as I zip past on my cool bicycle.

We're going to have so much fun,
and I'm not even done!

Together, we'll play hide-and-seek,
and I promise to count without one peek.

We'll play baseball and catch on the
playground outside,
and speed down the super-fast slide.

I'll even take you out to fish in the lake,
and then we'll create a one-of-a-kind
mud cake!

I can't wait for all these things with you,
but there's still so much to do!

Together we're going to read stories before bed
and make up silly songs in our head.

We're going to scare Daddy when he's not
looking, and sneak food
from Mommy when she is cooking.

We're going to celebrate special days and
spend holidays together always.

And as much as I love you, I know that there's
some trouble we'll get into!

If we play and fall into a muddy puddle, together
we'll give Mommy a slimy cuddle.

If we find cool creepy crawly bugs, we'll bring them
home and give them lots of hugs.

And if we get caught drawing on the table,
we will giggle but clean it as best as we're
able.

We have so much more fun ahead,
but there's still so much
I haven't said!

We'll run into Daddy's office and draw him
two hearts, then flee before he sees his new
art.

We'll play with my toys because they are cool,
and hide when
Mommy makes us get out of the pool

We'll play all day and play all night, even after
bedtime as we play by flashlight.

Little sibling, I promise to be your best friend, and I promise to play with you to no end.

I promise to be the best big brother ever, and I promise to love you forever.

I promise to help if you get into trouble, and I will always be there for you on the double.

So, what does it mean to be a big brother?

It means I love you like no other.

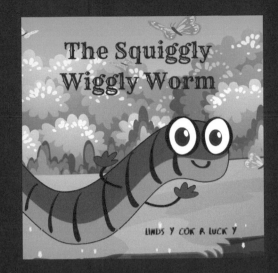

Reviews are so important for independently published authors. If you enjoyed the book, please take a minute to leave an Amazon review.
Thank you!

CPSIA information can be obtained
at www.ICGtesting.com
Printed in the USA
LVHW072353161219
640741LV00012B/339/P